**DREAMWORKS**

# THE BOSS BABY

## Junior Novelization

Based on the DreamWorks Animation movie
written by Michael McCullers
Adapted by Tracey West

Simon Spotlight
New York   London   Toronto   Sydney   New Delhi

SIMON SPOTLIGHT
An imprint of Simon & Schuster Children's Publishing Division
1230 Avenue of the Americas, New York, New York 10020
This Simon Spotlight edition February 2017
The Boss Baby © 2017 DreamWorks Animation LLC. All Rights Reserved.
All rights reserved, including the right of reproduction in whole or in part in any form.
SIMON SPOTLIGHT and colophon are registered trademarks of Simon & Schuster, Inc.
For information about special discounts for bulk purchases, please contact
Simon & Schuster Special Sales at 1-866-506-1949 or business@simonandschuster.com.
Designed by Nicholas Sciacca
The text of this book was set in Bodoni.
Manufactured in the United States of America 0317 OFF
10 9 8 7 6 5 4 3 2
ISBN 978-1-4814-9170-9 (hc)
ISBN 978-1-4814-7006-3 (pbk)
ISBN 978-1-4814-7007-0 (eBook)

# Chapter 1
# Just the Three of Us

My name is Tim, and this is my story. It starts when I was seven years old, and I relied on my imagination. Back then life was one big adventure after another. At least, that's how I remember it. It was just the three of us—the Templetons. Me, Mom, and Dad.

And Mom and Dad had lots of time to play with me.

I had the greatest parents ever—and they had the coolest jobs! They worked for the biggest pet company in the world: Puppy Co. They got to test out all the new products for puppies. Sometimes, they let me help.

But even though they were busy, they always had time for our adventures. Bath time was never just bath time—we would pretend we were swimming with sharks under the ocean!

And every night, we had our special bedtime ritual. Three stories. Five hugs. And finally, Mom and

Dad would sing my special song.

*"Little bird, don't you cry, one day you will learn to fly. . . ."*

When they finished singing, they would tuck me in and I would drift off to sleep, perfectly content. I was the star of the Templeton family show. The center of the universe.

Then one night something different happened. Mom and Dad read me three stories. They gave me five hugs. They sang the song. Then, before they tucked me in, Dad asked me, "Hey, Tim, how would you like to have a baby brother?"

"No thanks," I replied. "I'm enough."

Maybe I should have wondered why he asked me, but I didn't. Instead, as I drifted off to sleep, I wondered where babies came from. Long conveyor belts carried new babies around a big baby factory. The babies got diapers and booties. Then a machine arm tickled their tummies. The babies who giggled got sent down a chute with a blinking green sign that read: FAMILY.

I saw lots of babies giggle, one after the other.

Then one baby got tickled, but he didn't giggle at all! The sign turned red, and read: MANAGEMENT.

A flipper knocked the baby down a long, steep chute. His booties and pacifier flew off. He dropped down the chute into a pair of black pants. Then machine hands gave him a pair of loafers, a watch, and a jacket and tie!

A robotic suction-cup picked him up and dropped him into an office chair. The chair rolled down a long tube. A machine arm handed him a briefcase, and another arm handed him a bottle with a label that read: SUPER SECRET BABY FORMULA.

Then the office chair rolled into a room filled with cubicles, like in Mom and Dad's office. The baby in the suit slid behind the desk. Somehow, I knew what this strange baby was.

He was a Boss Baby.

When I woke up, I remembered the whole dream. I thought it was weird and then forgot about it, until a few weeks later.

That's when everything changed, and my weird dream became a real-live nightmare!

## Chapter 2
## Baby Invasion!

The day I got a brother started out like any other day, but little did I know that my life would never be the same. Wizzie—my alarm clock that looks like a wizard—woke me up.

"Wake up, little halflings! It's seven a.m.!"

I jumped down from my bed. "Morning, Wizzie!" I replied.

"What great adventure lies in wait for you today?" Wizzie asked.

I fished through the toys scattered around my room and pulled out a safari helmet. I grabbed my toy binoculars and ran to my window to look outside for dinosaurs. As I was scanning for prehistoric monsters, a taxi pulled up in front of my house and a baby in a suit carrying a briefcase stepped out. My parents always said that I had an overactive imagination, but I clearly remember that he was delivered in a taxi. He walked past my bicycle and kicked it over. Then he strutted excitedly up to the front door.

Suddenly I knew where I had seen that baby before—from my dream! It was the Boss Baby! He was real. But what was he doing at my house?

I ran downstairs and saw Mom and Dad standing there. Mom was holding Boss Baby in her arms, just like he was a normal baby. Then Dad smiled at me.

"Tim, meet your new baby brother," he said.

Baby brother? I couldn't believe what Dad had just said. I had a million questions. Who is this guy? Why's he here? What's with that outfit? Why is he so fat? Why's he staring at me? Does he know karate? What's going on?

But before I could ask any of them, Boss Baby started to cry. Mom and Dad tried to get the baby to stop crying. They had no clue that he was not a typical baby.

Right from the start he was yelling at people, ordering everyone around. One thing was clear, he was the boss.

*"Waaaaaaaaaaah!"*

He would cry, and they would bring him a bottle.

*"Waaaaaaaaaah!"*

Then he would slap the bottle right out of their hands!

*"Waaaaaaaaaah!"*

Mom and Dad would run and get him his favorite toy, Señor Squeaky. But he would slap that out of their hands too!

*"Waaaaaaaaaah!"*

He even bossed them around in the middle of the night! He didn't care if anyone needed to sleep. And pretty soon all his toys and baby things took over every room of the house. It was like some kind of alien invasion.

That Boss Baby had everyone wrapped around his chubby little finger—everyone except for me. I knew just what he was, but I had to convince Mom and Dad, somehow, that my new little brother was not a normal baby at all.

## Chapter 3
# What about Me?

One night Mom and Dad were feeding Boss Baby his dinner. He was being good for once. They took turns spooning the food into his mouth and wiping his face clean.

"Who's Mommy's little cutie?" Mom cooed.

"No, he's Daddy's little tough guy, right?" Dad asked. Then he looked at Mom. "You know, one of us has to go with Mr. Francis to the Pet Convention."

I was watching Boss Baby's face, and I could swear he understood every word they were saying. He looked very interested.

"Oh, the convention in Vegas," Mom said. "You know what, you should go."

"No, no, you should go," Dad said.

They both started arguing about who would get to stay home with the baby. Then Mom said, "Maybe the baby should decide."

7

She turned to him and started talking in a sweet, high-pitched baby voice. "Who do you want to stay with you? Daddy? Or *Mommy*?"

"Or *Daddy*!" Dad jumped in.

"He wants his mommy," Mom said.

I couldn't take it anymore. "Ugh! We need to talk. In private!" I demanded.

Mom and Dad looked at me. "About what, bud?" Dad asked.

I didn't want Boss Baby to know that I was onto him. "About the B-A-B-E-E," I spelled out.

Mom laughed. "*Y*, Tim."

"Why? Because he came out of nowhere. We don't even know him. How can we trust him?" I asked.

Mom shook her head. "Tim . . ."

At that moment, Boss Baby smacked his bowl and baby food flew right into Mom and Dad's faces! It was like he was trying to change the subject. But I wasn't giving up.

"Seriously, am I the only one who thinks there's something weird about this guy?" I asked.

I planted both hands on the table and leaned forward as I was making my point. Boss Baby yanked the tablecloth and I face-planted into my dinner plate! He was trying to silence me, I knew it!

I jumped out of my chair. "Look at him! He wears a suit!"

"I know. Isn't it cute?" Mom said. "He's like a little man."

"He carries a briefcase," I pointed out. "Doesn't anyone else think that's a little freaky?"

Dad smiled. "Well, you carried around Lam-Lam until you were like—"

I interrupted him. "This is not about Lam-Lam," I said, and Boss Baby snorted, like he thought that was funny or something.

Mom put on her gentle voice. "All babies are different, Tim," she said.

"And each one is special," Dad added.

"He's taking over the whole house!" I cried.

Mom looked at Boss Baby and smiled. "Are you taking over the whole house? Yes, you are! Yes, you are!"

That baby made adorable faces at Mom. But when she turned away, he looked right at me and nodded. He DID understand everything we were saying. I knew it!

"Trust me, one day you're going to get to know this little guy," Dad said as he kissed Boss Baby on the head. "And you're going to love him with all your heart. Just like we do."

"*All* your heart?" I asked, and I felt like my own heart was breaking.

If Mom and Dad had given all their hearts to Boss Baby, what was left for me?

## Chapter 4
# He Can Talk!

That night, I waited patiently in bed for my three stories, five hugs, and special song. I waited and waited, but Mom and Dad never came into my room.

I got out of bed and tiptoed down the hallway.

"Mom? Dad?" I whispered loudly.

I peeked inside their room. They were already asleep! They were tired out from being ordered around by Boss Baby.

I was thinking about waking them up when I heard a phone ring. It didn't sound like my Mom or Dad's cell phone, though. It had kind of a weird, high-pitched sound.

The ring was coming from the end of the hallway. I slowly made my way toward the sound. A light was glowing from inside Boss Baby's room! Then, the ringing stopped—and I heard a voice.

"I'm making great progress with the parents already," someone was saying in a deep voice. "Oh, the usual procedure. Sleep deprivation, hunger strikes. They're very disoriented. I've got them eating out of the palm of my hand. It's hilarious, but I think the kid might be onto me."

My heart was pounding as I opened the door to Boss Baby's room and peeked inside.

Somebody was in Boss Baby's room! At least that's what I thought. I slowly opened the door and peeked inside. Then I gasped.

Boss Baby was talking into a toy phone!

"No, I can handle him," Boss Baby was saying into the phone. "I know how important this mission is to the company.

*"Mission?"* I whispered. What exactly was this weird baby up to?

"Well, trust me, ma'am," Boss Baby said. "You got the right baby for this job."

I pushed open the door and hit the light switch.

"Hands up!" I shouted.

Boss Baby turned around.

"Fart! Poop! Doodie!" he said, trying to make me think he was a regular baby. But I knew better now.

"You can talk!" I said, pointing at him.

Boss Baby's eyes got wide, and I knew he was trying to look innocent. "Uh, goo-goo ga-ga."

"No. You can really talk. I heard you," I insisted.

Boss Baby nodded. "Fine. I can talk. Now let's see if you can listen. Get me a double espresso, and see if there's someplace around here with decent sushi. What I wouldn't do for a spicy tuna roll right about now."

He took some dollar bills from his diaper and tossed them at me.

"Get yourself a little something," he said.

I still couldn't believe he could talk. He sounded just like a grown-up. "Who are you?" I asked him.

"Let's just say . . . I'm the boss," he replied.

"But you're a baby. You wear a diaper," I pointed out.

Boss Baby walked over to the closet. He pushed aside a box of diapers, revealing a safe. He opened the safe and took out a bottle marked SUPER SECRET BABY FORMULA—just like I had seen in my dream.

"You know who else wears diapers?" he asked as he mixed himself a bottle of formula. "Astronauts and race-car drivers, that's who. It's called efficiency, Templeton. The average toddler spends what—forty-five hours a year on the potty? I'm the boss. I don't have that kind of spare time."

I folded my arms across my chest. "Well, you're not the boss of me."

"I *am* the boss of you," Boss Baby said.

"No, you're not," I shot back.

Boss Baby slapped my legs right out from under me, and I landed in a tiny plastic chair.

"Am too!" Boss Baby cried.

"Are not!" I said.

Boss Baby climbed onto his high chair. Then he squirted formula at me, and I dodged it.

"Am too!"

"Are not!"

"Am too!"

"Are not! I was here first!" I said in exasperation.

"Just wait till Mom and Dad find out about this."

Then Boss Baby stuck his stubby little finger right in my face.

"Oh yeah? You think they'd pick *you* over me? With your track record?" he asked.

"You don't know anything about me," I told him.

Boss Baby opened his briefcase and pulled out a folder. "So that's how you want to play it, huh? Let's see . . . Templeton, Timothy. Middle name . . . ha! I'm sorry. Your middle name is Leslie! Your grades are mostly C's."

I didn't like where this was going. "How do you know all that?" I asked.

But he didn't answer. "Says here you can't ride a bike without training wheels. Even bears can ride bikes without training wheels, Leslie."

"Um . . ." I didn't know what to say to that.

"Date of birth says you're seven," Boss Baby continued.

"Seven and a half," I corrected him.

Suddenly Boss Baby's eyes closed, and he started drooling and snoring. His head fell forward and hit the tray of his high chair. He woke right back up.

"Power nap! You were saying?" he asked.

"I'm seven and a half," I replied.

Boss Baby nodded. "Exactly. You're old. It's time to make way for the next generation. It's the way of the world. You would never ask your parents for an old toy."

He held out a stuffed lamb—*my* stuffed lamb.

"Lam-Lam!" I cried.

"Everyone wants the hot new thing," Boss Baby said. He picked up a robot toy and pretended to make it fight with Lam-Lam! Then he tossed both toys aside. I caught Lam-Lam and held her close to me.

"Mom and Dad don't even *know* you," I told him. "They *love* me."

"Oh yeah?" Boss Baby said. "Do the math, kid. There's only so much love to go around. It's like . . . these beads."

Boss Baby picked up one of his toys and put it in front of me. It was a row of colorful beads that you could slide back and forth on a rod. Boss Baby pushed all the beads to the left side and said, "You used to have all your parents' love, all their time, all their attention. You had all the beads. But then I came along."

"Babies take a lot of time," he added. He slid two beads over the right.

"They need a lot of attention," he said. He slid three more beads over to the right.

"They get all the love," he finished, and he slid all the beads over to the right! There were no more beads on my side.

"We could share," I suggested.

"You obviously didn't go to business school," Boss Baby said. "Look, Templeton. The numbers just don't add up. There's not enough love for the two of us. Not enough beads to go around. And then, all of a sudden, there's no place for Tim! Tim doesn't fit anymore. So keep quiet, stay out of my way, or there's gonna be cutbacks."

I didn't like what Boss Baby was saying.

"You can't be fired from your own family," I said, but I wasn't sure if I believed my own words.

I left Boss Baby's room and went back to bed. I fell asleep with no stories, no hugs, and no song.

I only had one thought: *What if you could be fired from your family?*

## Chapter 5
# Boss Baby's Playdate

The next morning Wizzie the alarm clock went off like he always did.

"Wake up, little halflings! It's seven a.m.!"

"What's the use," I said to myself, and to my surprise, Wizzie answered my question.

"What's wrong, Timothy? Has that little dwarf made you blue?"

I nodded.

"Then I shall cast upon him a great curse!" Wizzie promised.

"It's no use, Wizzie," I explained. "He's got Mom and Dad fooled. If they knew what I knew, they'd never let him stay."

"Perhaps your parents need to be enlightened," Wizzie suggested.

"Yeah, I need to enlighten them," I said, and then I suddenly realized what Wizzie was trying to tell me. "That's what I need—proof!"

"Expose his dark magic," Wizzie encouraged.

Suddenly, I felt a whole lot better. I had a plan! All I had to do was prove to my parents that Boss Baby wasn't a real baby. Then they would send him back to the baby store (or whatever they called that weird place he came from).

I jumped out of bed, grabbed a microphone and recorder, loaded a cassette tape inside the recorder, and put on my spy gear, complete with spy glasses, a mask, and mittens. I made my way down the hallway, moving like a ninja, stealthily flipping and leaping to the staircase. Everything was going so smoothly until I stepped on one of the baby's toys and tripped and tumbled down the stairs. As I rubbed my aching back, I was surrounded by babies!

I screamed. "They're spreading!"

One of them was the biggest baby I had ever seen. I tried to get up, but he pinned me to the ground. I watched in horror as spit drooled out of his mouth, dangling closer and closer to my face. Then, out of the corner of my eye, I saw a three-headed baby

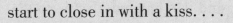

start to close in with a kiss. . . .

Just then Mom and Dad walked into the room.

"Mom? Dad? What's going on? It's an invasion!" I cried.

"It's a playdate," Mom replied, and Dad snapped a photo of the babies with his camera. Then they went into the kitchen to show the picture to the other babies' parents.

Boss Baby waddled up to me. "It's a *meeting*. And you won't be attending."

Then he marched off into the living room, followed by the other babies. I saw that the three-headed baby was really triplets. What was Boss Baby up to now?

"We'll see about that," I said.

A few minutes later, I was hidden behind the big plant in the living room. The babies didn't see me. I stuck the microphone into the plant. I was finally going to get my proof!

The babies were sitting on the floor, around the coffee table.

"Thank you for coming here on such short

notice," Boss Baby said. He handed a rattle to the big baby, Jimbo, who started shaking it, so I could no longer get any good sound through the microphone. I moved into a better hiding position.

Boss Baby started his speech again. "We babies are having a crisis."

"Oh no!" said one triplet.

"That's awful!" said the second triplet.

"Horrible!" said the third triplet.

"What is it?" another baby named Staci asked.

"Well, it's simpler if I just show you," Boss Baby said. He picked up a teddy bear. "Teddy, if you please."

The bear's head tilted back revealing a projector.

"Jimbo, hit the lights," Boss Baby said, and the big baby knocked over the lamp, breaking it. Then a beam shone from the projector and a picture appeared on the living room wall.

"You see, babies aren't getting as much love as we used to," Boss Baby said.

"Why? Have we been bad?" Staci asked.

"No, Staci. But I'll tell you who is," Boss Baby

said as a picture of a cute puppy flashed on the wall.

"Behold, our mortal enemy: puppies!" Boss Baby cried.

All the babies thought the puppy was cute. "Awwwwwwwwww!"

"No! No! That's exactly the problem," Boss Baby said. "Throughout history, people have loved babies more than anything in the world. Puppies were merely . . . accessories. But that all changed when the puppies began coming out in designer models, each one more adorable than the last. Remember the Labradoodle? The Peekapoo? The Chiweenie? Try to say Chiweenie without smiling."

"Chi-wee . . ." the babies began.

"Not possible. Don't waste your time," he snapped. "And things are getting even worse. Francis Francis, the CEO of Puppy Co., made this announcement. Teddy, roll the clip."

Francis Francis is Mom and Dad's boss. Teddy was projecting a video of him on the wall. Francis Francis was standing in front of a microphone.

Puppies ran around him, nipping at his feet.

"Puppy Co. is about to release the most adorable puppy ever," Francis said. "We're going to launch it at the Pet Convention in Las Vegas!"

Las Vegas. Mom and Dad had been talking about going there, I remembered.

"It's gonna crush the competition!" Francis Francis said, and the video ended. Jimbo started to clap.

Boss Baby stood in front of the screen. "No, Jimbo. *We* are the competition. This is war! Puppies are winning and babies are losing. And if this new puppy is as cute as we fear, it could put the baby business out of business, baby."

"Uh-oh," said the first triplet.

"That's awful," said the second triplet.

"Bad news, B.B.," said the third triplet.

"What are we going to do?" Staci asked, worried.

"My job is to find out exactly what this new puppy is so that Baby Corp. can stop it—and you're going to help me," Boss Baby replied.

The babies all cheered.

"Now, I've selected you because your parents all work for Puppy Co. So, have you learned anything about the new puppy from them?" Boss Baby asked.

Jimbo clapped his hands. "Yaaaay! Puppy!"

Boss Baby frowned. "No, Jimbo, puppies are evil," he said. "Staci, read back the notes."

"I can't read," Staci said. She showed the babies the notepad she had been scribbling on. There was a mess of wiggly lines. "What's it say?"

Jimbo didn't answer. He shook his rattle and danced around.

Boss Baby grabbed the rattle from Jimbo. "This is my team? A muscle-head, a bunch of yes men, and a doodler?"

"Exactly!" said the first triplet.

"Affirmative!" said the second triplet.

"Good call, B.B.!" said the third triplet.

That's when I realized something. Jimbo's rattle was quiet, and I was getting great sound in my headphones!

"Put that cookie down," I heard Boss Baby say to Jimbo. "Cookies are for closers."

25

I grinned. I had the proof I needed that this was no ordinary baby!

Meanwhile, Teddy started talking. "There's plenty of love to go around!" he declared in his recorded voice.

"Teddy! Go to sleep," Boss Baby commanded, ripping out the toy's batteries.

Then the three triplets called out in alarm.

"Boss!"

"Boss!"

"Boss!"

"What?" Boss Baby yelled.

"Parents!" the triplets said together.

Mom and Dad came into the room with the parents of the other babies. I was still hiding. All the babies, even Boss Baby, started acting like normal babies, rolling on the floor, drooling, babbling, and doing all the other things that adults seem to think is cute. The parents loved it and they started taking pictures.

Then Dad looked at the other parents. "Now, who's hungry?"

After the parents left, Boss Baby made a face. "Gah, this is so humiliating!"

I rewound the tape to make sure I had gotten it.

*"Gah, this is so humiliating!"*

It was perfect! "Wait till Mom and Dad hear this," I said under my breath.

I jumped out of my hiding place, planning to make a beeline to the kitchen—and found myself facing a wall of angry babies.

"Hey, Templeton, whatcha got there?" Boss Baby asked.

"Uh, nothing," I said innocently.

Boss Baby glared at me. "Hand over the tape," he demanded.

"Never!" I cried, and I turned and ran out the front door.

## Chapter 6
# The Chase Is On!

I ran outside, around the house, and into the back-yard. Through the glass door to our kitchen, I saw all the parents gathered around the table.

"Mom! Dad! Out here!" I yelled.

They saw me, but they just waved.

I ran toward the door to open it, but the babies rolled right in front of me in their toy vehicles! Staci was riding a motorcycle. The triplets were in a toy fire engine. Jimbo was pushing one of those bubbles filled with little balls that pop like corn when the wheels turn.

"You can't get away from Johnny Law, Simpleton!" Boss Baby said from the driver's seat of his minia-ture police car.

The babies rolled right toward me! I ran to the sandbox. I got through it easily, but the wheels of Staci's motorcycle got stuck. Jimbo chased me with his popping thing as I ran to the chain-link fence at the back of the yard. I bounced off the fence, but big ol' Jimbo broke right through it!

I thought I was in the clear, but the triplets wheeled up to me, and one of them snatched the tape recorder right out of my hands! I had to think fast. I grabbed the fire hose on the truck and wrapped it around the base of the sprinkler. The hose caused the fire truck to stop short and the tape recorder went flying out of one of the triplets' hands.

Jimbo picked up the triplets, just before the fire truck exploded!

"Whoa!" I cried out. Then Boss Baby whizzed through the smoke in his police car. He snatched the tape recorder out of the air. I grabbed onto the bumper of the car to slow him down, and he dragged me across the lawn. He made a hard turn, and I lost my grip. I went tumbling across the grass.

Boss Baby held up the tape recorder and started to laugh maniacally, taunting me with his victory, and before I could go after him, Jimbo and the triplets came running right at me!

I grabbed the rope that dangles down from my pirate tree house, and the rope pulled me up onto the platform.

"Oooh," the triplets cooed. Even they knew it was cool.

Luckily, I had a toy in my tree house that shoots foam darts. I grabbed on to the zip line stretching from my tree house to a tree across the yard, and as I whizzed down the line, I shot foam darts at Boss Baby.

"You wanna play? Let's play!" I challenged.

"Noooo! Save Boss!" Jimbo yelled, and he ran in front of Boss Baby to block the attack. Foam darts hit every part of his big baby body.

Scared, Boss Baby threw the tape recorder and it landed right at my feet. I didn't question my luck. I picked it up and just started running.

"Grab him!" Boss Baby yelled, and Staci and the triplets chased after me. They were fast for babies!

That's when I made a bold move. Please don't try this at home. I jumped on the backyard trampoline, so high that I could dive right through the open window into the upstairs hallway! I was pretty impressed with myself. I poked my head out of the window and held up the tape recorder.

"You're toast, baby man!" I yelled down.

Boss Baby tugged on Jimbo's arm. "Upsies! I need upsies!"

Jimbo picked up Boss Baby and did something you should never do. He tossed Boss Baby like a football. Jimbo was aiming for the open window, but instead Boss Baby crashed through a glass window!

That's when Dad and Mom walked outside and found Staci and Jimbo crying and the triplets bouncing on the trampoline. I didn't know that yet, because I was running toward the stairs as fast as I could.

"Mom! Dad! I've got proof!" I yelled.

Boss Baby climbed into his exersaucer. He rolled after me, but I reached the stairs first. I jumped on the bannister and slid down. Boss Baby skidded to a stop.

"Oh, someone can't go down the stairs?" I taunted him. "Ha!"

Boss Baby got a fierce look in his eyes. "Nothing can stop me!" he yelled. Then he did something very unsafe—he rolled down the stairs in his exersaucer!

I opened the front door and when Boss Baby reached the bottom of the stairs, he rolled right out the door! I slammed it behind him.

"Mom! Dad!" I yelled. I ran into the kitchen, but nobody was there. I checked the living room, but that was empty too. Then I ran into Dad's office.

"Mom! Dad! The baby can talk!" I cried.

Dad's desk chair swung around, but he wasn't in it. Boss Baby was in the chair! And he was holding Lam-Lam—and a stapler.

"Hand over the tape, Timmy," Boss Baby demanded. "Or Lam-Lam gets it!"

## Chapter 7
# I'm in Big Trouble

"No!" I yelled.

Boss Baby ignored me. "What's that, Lam-Lam?" he asked. "You want a nose ring?"

Boss Baby punched a staple into Lam-Lam's nose.

"Ah!" I yelled.

"And an eyebrow ring?" Boss Baby asked. "How's that going to look in a job interview?"

He punched another staple above Lam-Lam's eye! It was horrible!

I took the cassette tape out of the tape recorder. I couldn't bear to see Lam-Lam get stapled. I looked at the tape in my hands. It was the only proof I had.

Boss Baby started to pull on Lam-Lam's arms. "The tape, Timmy, or I'm gonna rip, rip, rip . . ."

I didn't want to give the tape to Boss Baby. But I didn't want to lose Lam-Lam, either. I lunged forward, grabbing Lam-Lam's head. I had a tug-of-war with Boss Baby. I pulled, he pulled, and poor Lam-Lam's head ripped right off!

I was furious. I picked up Boss Baby and marched him into the living room. Then I plopped him into his bouncy baby jumper.

"Templeton, let's be reasonable," Boss Baby said, and he sounded nervous. "What are you doing?"

"You've been asking for this since you got here," I told him as I rolled him toward the open living room window.

"We can talk about this over a juice box!" Boss Baby pleaded.

"The time for juice boxes is over," I said firmly. "Say bye-bye, baby. You're fired!"

Then I heard my Dad's voice. "Tim, what are you doing?"

I spun around quickly, letting go of the bouncer. "Nothing," I said innocently.

But Boss Baby was a fast thinker. He grabbed onto my shirt. *Whoosh!* The tape flew out the window, onto the street, and a car ran over it.

"My proof!" I yelled, running to the window.

Mom picked up Boss Baby. The other parents walked in, holding their babies. Everyone looked at me like I was some kind of monster.

"Tim, explain yourself," Mom said, in her calm-but-mad voice.

"It wasn't me," I protested. "It was the baby's fault!"

"The baby's fault?" Dad asked.

"It's true!" I blurted out. "He can talk. They can all talk. They were having a meeting. Something about puppies."

"Timothy Leslie Templeton," Mom said, using my middle name—so I knew she was really angry. And I saw Boss Baby smirk when she said it.

"We are very disappointed in you," Dad said.

"No, we're mad at you," Mom corrected him.

"Mad?" I asked.

Dad nodded. "You need a time out."

"You're grounded!" Mom said, looking at Dad.

Dad agreed with her. "Yes, grounded . . . for two—"

"Three weeks!" Mom finished.

I couldn't believe my ears. "Grounded?"

"You're going to stay in this house with your baby brother until you learn to get along," Mom said.

I groaned. I couldn't imagine a worse punishment in the entire world!

That night, I stared at the bare walls of my cell. What had once been my bedroom was now a jail and I was sentenced to solitary confinement. Outside the cell, I could hear people enjoying life. I could hear them singing. . . .

*"Little bird, don't you cry, one day you will learn to fly. . . ."*

"Hey, that's my song," I said sadly. And Mom and Dad weren't singing it to me. I slumped down into bed.

Wizzie tried to help. "It's okay, little halfling. Perhaps I could be of some assistance."

Wizzie started to sing, but the words were all wrong.

"Thanks, Wizzie, but it's not the same," I told him.

"If only I could break us out of this big house," Wizzie said in support.

A few minutes later, I heard someone whispering at my door.

"Templeton, we have to talk." It was Boss Baby!

"Go away!" I hissed.

Boss Baby crawled into the room. He hopped onto my toy train and it carried him toward my bed. Then he started to sing in his weird grown-up voice.

*"Little bird, don't you cry . . ."*

I sat up. "Stop it!" I told him. "That's my song. My parents wrote it just for me, and you stole it! You're trying to steal everything from me, even my parents! You're the one who should be in jail."

The train stopped. "Look, it's time we put our differences aside."

I couldn't answer him. I was sniffling from crying. Boss Baby noticed.

"Hey, have you been—"

"No!" I said. I didn't want that baby to see me cry.

Boss Baby climbed onto the bed. He put his hand on my shoulder. Then he held out a wad of money.

"Take it," he said.

I pushed it away. "I don't want your filthy money."

"Look, I told you to stay out of my way," Boss Baby said.

"I can't," I replied. "You're in *my* house."

"I don't want you to be here anymore than you want me to be here," Boss Baby said.

"Then why are you torturing me?" I asked.

Boss Baby leaned closer to me. "Well, the truth is, I'm no ordinary baby."

"Well, no kidding," I said.

"I'm on a mission from above," he said. "I'm middle management for the company."

"The company? What company?" I asked, although I suspected it had something to do with my dream.

Boss Baby reached into his pocket and pulled out a blue pacifier. He handed it to me. "Take this. It'll explain everything."

I eyed the pacifier suspiciously. "What do you want me to do with that?"

"It's for you to suck," he replied.

I made a face. "Yuck! I'm not sucking that. I don't know where it's been."

"It's not where it's been. It's where it will take you," Boss Baby said, and then he put the pacifier in my hand. "Don't you want to know where babies really come from?"

I have to admit, I was curious. My dream hadn't told me much. If I wanted to get rid of Boss Baby, I needed to find out everything I could about him.

Boss Baby pulled out a red pacifier.

"Binky. Boo-Boo. Nuk-Nuk. It goes by many names, but through its power you will know the truth," he said.

He had convinced me. He popped the red pacifier into his mouth, and I popped the blue one into mine. Then we both sucked our pacifiers, faster and faster, until a swirling vortex appeared and sucked us both inside!

## Chapter 8
## Welcome to Baby Corp!

I screamed as the vortex pulled me out of my bed, up through the roof of my house, and then up, up, up, into the clouds. Through the clouds I saw a tall glass building shaped like an enormous baby bottle and toy blocks. The vortex dropped us onto a plaza in front of the building. I landed on the ground with a thud while Boss Baby floated down peacefully.

I stood up and looked around me. Crowds of babies, all dressed in business suits, were hurrying across the plaza into the building.

"Whoa . . . where are we?" I asked.

"Welcome to Baby Corp.," Boss Baby said.

Baby Corp. . . . . It definitely reminded me of the place in my dream, except all these babies were business babies. Some of them hopped across the plaza on bouncy balls. Others rolled across the plaza, riding toys on wheels.

Not far away, I saw a counter with a long slide next to it. A baby slid down the slide and landed on the counter. The baby behind the counter handed him a bottle marked SUPER SECRET BABY FORMULA.

As I was watching this, a baby businessman walked right through me, like a ghost!

"Ah!" I screamed.

"Relax," Boss Baby said. "They can't see or hear us."

"We're like, virtual and stuff?" I asked, and Boss Baby confirmed. I guess that's why I no longer had a pacifier in my mouth. My virtual self didn't need it.

Boss Baby led me into the lobby of the big, glass baby-bottle-shaped building.

"So this is where babies come from?" I asked.

"Of course. What did you think? The stork? Magic fairies?" Boss Baby said.

I shook my head. "I can't believe my parents didn't tell me about this."

"If people knew where babies really came from, they'd never have one," he explained. "Same thing with hot dogs, by the way."

I followed him to the elevator. I had to duck, because it was made for baby-sized people.

"Going upsies!" the elevator announced, and the doors closed and we began to rise.

Something occurred to me. "How come I don't remember this place?"

"After normal babies get their pacifiers taken away, they forget all about Baby Corp.," Boss Baby answered. "A few of us are selected for the ultimate honor. . . ."

*Ding!* The elevator doors opened and we stepped into a room filled with cubicles, just like the room from my dream. Babies in suits were already hard at work.

"Upper management!" Boss Baby said proudly. I followed him down a row of cubicles. "This is where all the action is."

"So this whole place is run by babies?" I asked, looking around to see if there were any grown-ups in sight.

Then an announcement came over the speakers. *"Nap time in Sector G."*

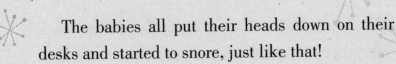

The babies all put their heads down on their desks and started to snore, just like that!

Another question occurred to me. "What happens when you grow up?"

"Well, we don't," Boss Baby answered. "We drink a super secret baby formula that keeps us babies forever."

He nodded toward the water cooler, where a bunch of babies were drinking their bottles. One baby chugged his super secret baby formula, burped, and they all laughed.

Then another baby in a suit marched up to them, and she looked angry.

"Formula break is over! Back to work! We're in a crisis here!" she barked.

Another baby handed her a phone, and she started screaming into it.

"Who is that?" I asked.

"That's my boss. The Big Boss Baby," Boss Baby replied.

"What is she screaming about?" I wondered.

Boss Baby guided me over to a big screen with

a pie chart on it—that's a chart that looks like a pie, and each of the pieces stands for something different.

"This pie chart represents all the love there is in the world," Boss Baby explained. He pointed to one of the biggest slices on the chart. "The puppies' slice is getting bigger and bigger. They're stealing all our love!"

I understood. "Just like you did to me!"

"Exactly," Boss Baby said. "And if this keeps up there might not be enough pie left for babies."

"No pie!" I said.

Boss Baby shook his head solemnly. "No pie . . ."

He motioned for me to follow him and walked through a wall. Now we were in a room with lots of wood on the walls and fancy furniture.

"When I find out what Puppy Co.'s new puppy is, I'll be a Baby Corp. legend," Boss Baby told me. He pointed to a picture on the wall of a fat, grumpy-looking baby in a suit. "Like him."

"Now that's a big, fat baby," I said.

"No, *that's* Big Fat Boss Baby," he said, pointing

to a different picture. "*This* is Super Colossal Big Fat Boss Baby. He was the youngest Chief Executive Infant in the history of the company."

"Was? What happened to him?" I asked.

"Retired, years ago," Boss Baby replied. "But I still try to live up to his legend."

I was confused. "So that's all you get? Your picture on the wall?"

Boss Baby turned and walked through the wall again. I followed him into a big, empty office with a very high, high chair. "I'll get a big promotion. The corner office. With my own private potty."

"So when you're done, you're coming back here?" I asked.

"I'm not a family man," he said. "I belong behind a desk."

I smiled. "That's awesome!" The wheels in my head were slowly turning. . . .

We walked through the wall back into the hallway, and Big Boss Baby walked past us, followed by a whole group of baby assistants. She was yelling into her phone. "Did you hear anything from that little Boss Baby that we sent down to the Templetons? No? You're fired!"

She ended the call and turned to her assistants. "You ALL are fired!"

The babies ran away and a new group of baby assistants ran up to Big Boss Baby.

"The Pet Convention is in two days!" she yelled. "If he doesn't come up with answers, he's fired. Retired! He's gone!"

Boss Baby got a panicked look on his face.

"Okay, tour's over," he told me. In real life, he pulled the pacifier out of my mouth.

*Whoosh!* The vortex came back, sucked us up, and dropped us back into my house.

Boss Baby paced back and forth. "The Pet Convention is in two days and I've got nothing!" he wailed.

Then his toy phone rang.

"That's Big Boss Baby! Don't answer it!"

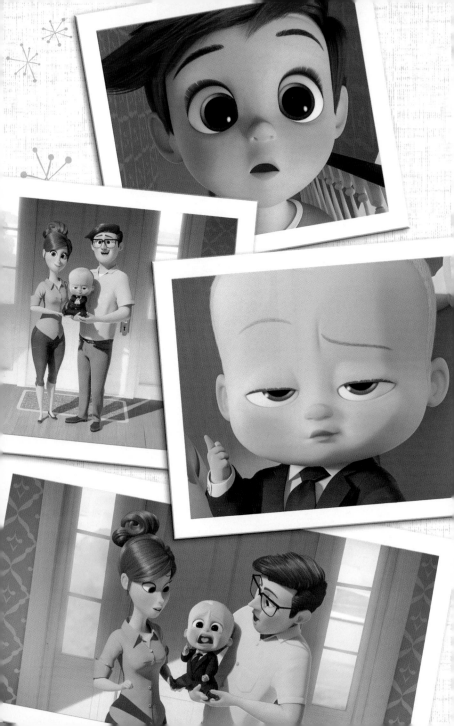

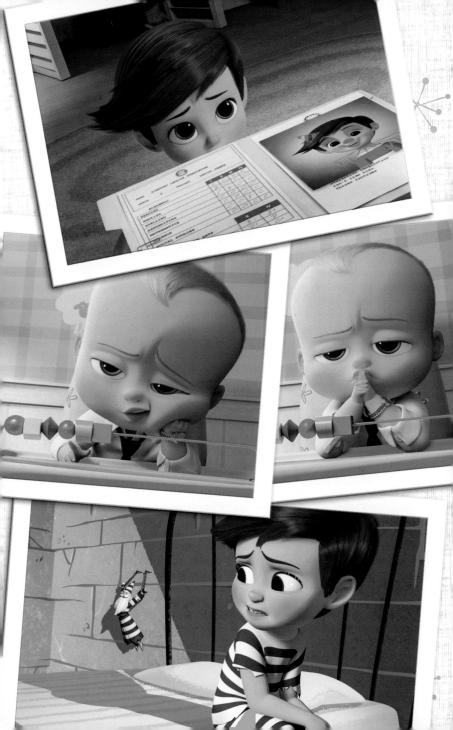

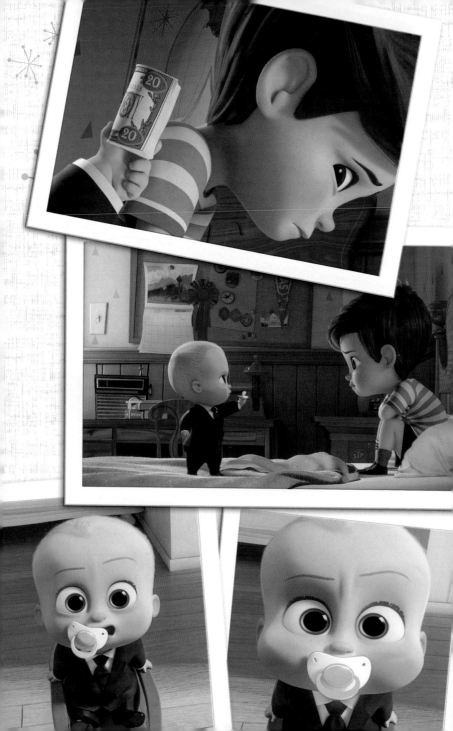

# Chapter 9
## We Make a Deal

Boss Baby tossed the ringing phone at me.

"Ahhh!" I screamed. I ducked, and the phone flew into the dirty diaper bin.

Boss Baby suddenly fell asleep, snored, and then just as suddenly snapped awake.

"Ah! Stress nap!" he cried. He picked up his Señor Squeaky toy and paced back and forth across the room. "If I don't find out what the new puppy is and fast, not only will I *not* get that promotion, I could get fired!"

He threw the toy across the room.

"Hey, relax," I told him. "I'm sure there's other cool jobs for babies, right? Meanwhile, two days goes by like that." I snapped my fingers. "You'd better start packing."

Boss Baby picked up the toy again and chucked it at me. "You don't get it, Templeton!" He grabbed me by my shirt collar. "If I'm fired, they'll take away my formula! I'll turn into a normal baby and then live here forever with you."

*Forever.* The word hit me like a brick. "No," I said.

Boss Baby nodded. "Every morning you wake up, I'll be there." I pictured rolling over in my bed in the morning. The first thing I saw was Boss Baby. For some reason he was dressed like Lam-Lam.

"Every night at dinner, I'll be there." I imagined Boss Baby's face staring up at me from my soup bowl.

"Every birthday party." I saw tiny Boss Babies pour out of a piñata.

"Every Christmas. I'll be there." I stared in horror at Boss Baby's face reflecting in every ornament on the tree.

"Year after year. We'll grow old together."

I could picture it in my mind: the two of us, old and wrinkled, fighting each other with our canes.

"We'll be brothers. Always," he finished.

"No! This is terrible!" I cried. "You can't stay here!"

Boss Baby didn't like the idea either. "I can't!"

"We have to fix this," I said. "We have to make sure you don't get fired."

"We?" Boss Baby asked.

I knew what I had to do. I picked up Boss Baby.

"We," I said firmly. "I will help you. But just to get rid of you. Deal?"

"Deal," Boss Baby said. "Here's to never seeing you again."

"Back atcha, baby!" I said.

We tried to shake hands, but it was weird because my hand was so much bigger than his.

"Now let's get to work," Boss Baby said.

We had to move fast. Boss Baby said we had to look through my parents' work files to get information about the new puppy. I knew that would be easy. I carried Boss Baby down to the living room. Both of my parents had fallen asleep on the couch, in the middle of doing work stuff. Boxes of open takeout food were scattered on the coffee table, along with all their Puppy Co. files.

It was perfect. I put on my Sherlock Holmes

hat and used a magnifying glass to read through Mom and Dad's papers. While I worked, Boss Baby played with our toy golf set.

I put down the page I was reading. "Ugh. There's nothing in here about a new puppy," I told him. "Aren't you going to do any work?"

"I'm very busy delegating," Boss Baby said, swinging his golf club.

"So once we find the file on the new puppy, what do you do then? Send in the baby ninjas?" I asked.

"Even better," Boss Baby said. "I'm going to write the perfect memo!"

"What's a memo?" I asked.

"A memo is something you write to give people information," he explained.

"That's your plan? You're going to write a book report? That's so boring!" I complained.

"No, Templeton, memos are for important things. A memo can bring people together. A memo can be a manifesto, a poem. A memo can change the world," Boss Baby said.

"Wow," I said sarcastically. "When you explain

it like that . . . it still sounds boring."

"You'll learn, kid. You'll learn," he said as he waddled over to the coffee table and picked up a slice of pizza from the take-out Mom and Dad had ordered. I shook my head and picked up another folder. A flier slipped out.

"Wait a second. This is it!" I cried.

"What is it?" Boss Baby asked.

I held up the flier. "Check it out. It's for Puppy Co.'s Take Your Kid to Work Day."

Boss Baby grimaced. "People take children to a place of business? Why?"

"Because it's awesome!" I told him.

"It's disgusting!" Boss Baby said with his mouth full of pizza.

"Don't you see?" I explained. "We can get inside Puppy Co. and find out what the new puppy is!"

Boss Baby put the pizza slice in a folder, put the folder in his briefcase, and then locked it. Then he grabbed an open cartoon of noodles from the coffee table.

"What's the point?" he asked. "You're grounded.

Your parents aren't going to take us anywhere." He slurped up a long noodle.

"You're right," I admitted. "They think we hate each other."

"'Hate' is a strong word," Boss Baby said. "It's the *right* word, but still."

"We have to convince them that we're actual brothers," I said. "That we l-l-l-l-l . . ." I still couldn't bring myself to say the word.

"Like?" Boss Baby guessed.

"No," I said. "That we l-l-l-l-l-l . . ."

"La la la?" Boss Baby asked.

I finally said it. "No. That we love each other."

Boss Baby gagged and noodle came out of his nose. He sniffed it back up.

"I just threw up a noodle and swallowed it," he said, disgusted with himself.

I'm not going to lie. It would be hard work having to pretend we loved each other. But we had to do it. If we didn't, Boss Baby would get fired and be stuck as my little brother forever. And neither of us wanted that!

So the next day, we started our plan at breakfast. I got Boss Baby in his high chair before Mom and Dad woke up and started to feed him.

"Here comes the choo choo train!" I said in a silly voice. "Choo choo! Chugga chugga!"

"No! Hold the train! It looks like it's already been eaten!" Boss Baby complained.

He chucked his sippy cup at me, just as Mom and Dad walked in.

"What's going on in here?" Mom asked.

"I'm just feeding the baby," I said innocently.

Mom and Dad looked suspicious, so I turned to Boss Baby. "They're watching," I whispered. Boss Baby frowned, but he knew what he had to do. "Choo choo!" I said again.

I held out the spoon. Boss Baby ate his baby food. Then he smiled.

Mom and Dad bought it.

"Okay," they said, and then left the kitchen. That's when Boss Baby spit the food right back in my face!

"Choo choo on that!" he said.

Later that day, I tried to put a sailor suit on Boss Baby. He hated the idea. He was fighting me and kicking me when Mom and Dad walked in.

"Tim! What are you doing?" Dad asked.

Boss Baby stopped kicking. I picked him up and showed them the sailor suit.

"Isn't he adorable?" I said.

Mom loved it. "Aw, and I've got one for you too! Ahoy, matey!"

"What?" I asked.

The next thing I knew, I was wearing a sailor suit that matched Boss Baby's! Mom and Dad took us to a photographer to get our picture taken. It was so humiliating! The photographer wanted us to smile but Boss Baby wouldn't do it, so I tickled him. He said he wasn't ticklish, but I found his tickle spot!

The photo looked pretty good, because we were both smiling and laughing in it. Mom and Dad ate it up.

That night we kept up the routine and I brought Boss Baby into the big recliner in the living room with me and read him a story.

"You should have seen your face in the picture," I told him. "You made such a crazy face!"

"I'm not used to being tickled," Boss Baby said.

"What? You've never been tickled? What about your parents?" I asked.

Boss Baby looked away and I realized something.

"I'm sorry, I forgot," I said. "You didn't have parents, did you?"

He turned to me. "Tim, I may look like a baby, but I was born all grown up."

"You never had someone to love you?" I asked.

Boss Baby shrugged. "Well, you can't miss what you never had."

For the first time, I felt bad for the little guy. He leaned in to me and fell asleep.

I felt my eyes get heavy. There was something about Boss Baby's soft breathing that was hypnotizing. I fell asleep.

I guess we must have looked pretty cute. Like real brothers who loved each other.

Our plan was working!

## Chapter 10
# Inside Puppy Co.

"Wake up, little halflings!"

The next thing I knew, I was in my own bed and Wizzie the alarm clock was waking me up. I opened my eyes and saw Dad leaning over me.

"Hey, Tim. Wake up, buddy!"

I rubbed my eyes. "Is something wrong? Am I fired?"

I could see Mom behind Dad, and they were both smiling.

"No!" Dad replied. "You're late for work!"

I was confused. "What?"

"It's Take Your Kid to Work Day! And you're the kid," Dad explained.

"You're officially ungrounded," Mom added.

I sat up. "Really?"

"Really," Dad said.

"Can the baby come too?" I asked.

Mom nodded. "I don't see why not."

I leaped out of bed. "Yes! Yes! Yes!"

"I wish I was that excited for work," Dad remarked.

Mom and Dad left me to get dressed. I couldn't believe it! Our plan had worked! I put on my clothes and rushed to tell Boss Baby. He was pretty happy. I helped him get dressed, and he stashed a bottle of his super secret baby formula in my backpack. Then we both put on sunglasses and looked in the mirror—we looked pretty cool, just perfect for our top-secret mission.

After breakfast, Mom and Dad packed us into the minivan and drove to Puppy Co. It wasn't my first time there. I recognized the main building, which was shaped like a giant barn. Behind it, a bunch of tall buildings stretched into the sky.

"Welcome to Puppy Co., gentlemen!" Dad announced as we pulled up.

The place was pretty crowded with Puppy Co. workers and their kids. The outside courtyard was filled with all kinds of kid-friendly activities. There was a ride with puppy-shaped cars that looped around and around on a track. There were carnival games where you could win a puppy plushy. Instead of a ball pen filled with colorful balls, there was an inflatable pool filled with stuffed puppies.

"Wow, this is awesome," I said as I pushed Boss Baby in his stroller through the courtyard.

Dad pointed toward a guy walking around in a puppy suit. The suit looked strange, and the guy inside it was laughing in a weird way.

"Hey, you want to get a picture with Puppy Co. Pete?" Dad asked.

"No, thanks," I said quickly. "It's probably too scary for the baby."

"Nice call," Boss Baby whispered to me.

Mom leaned over to me. "So, Tim, your Dad and I have some work to do. You want to come up to the office and hang out with us?"

"We'll stick your brother in the Puppy Zone while we have a little Tim time," Dad said. He nodded toward the entrance to the big room where all the little kids stayed for the day. The entrance looked like the face of a big, happy puppy.

"Look, Dad and I know we haven't been able to do as much with you as we used to," Mom said.

It was just what I wanted! It was so tempting, but I had to keep my sights on my goal: getting Boss Baby out of my life forever.

"No thanks," I said, trying to sound sincere. "I'd rather spend time with the baby."

"Oh, that's so cute!" Dad said.

I started to push the stroller.

"Way to keep your eyes on the prize, Templeton," Boss Baby whispered. "We pull this off and I go home."

"You guys stay in the Puppy Zone, okay?" Dad said.

"Okay, bye," I said—but I didn't mean it.

Mom and Dad watched as I pushed Boss Baby through the mouth of the giant puppy head, into the Puppy Zone. When we were inside, Boss Baby and I looked at each other.

It was time for our mission to begin.

First, we scoped out the place. I spotted a door

marked AUTHORIZED PERSONNEL ONLY, and I knew that meant the door would take us inside Puppy Co. I ditched the stroller, and Boss Baby and I crawled under a game booth so we could scout it out.

A security guard stood next to the door, making sure no kids opened it. But at his feet, there was a doggy door. Real puppies were going into and out of the door.

"We've got to get in so that we can find the secret file on the new puppy," I told Boss Baby.

"We'll never get through that door," he said.

I pointed to the doggy door. "Not that door, the doggy door," I said.

"But how do we get past the guard?" Boss Baby asked.

I looked up into the game booth we were hiding in. It was one of those games where you toss a ball at a row of dummies, and if you knock one down, you get a prize. The prizes were all plush puppies, clipped to strings that dangled down from the top of the game booth.

I pulled down one of the plush puppies. It was

the same size as Boss Baby. I held it out to him and waved the plush puppy's arms.

Boss Baby shook his head. "No way!" he protested.

Then I took the stuffing out of the puppy toy and dressed Boss Baby in the plush puppy skin. I know it sounds weird, but the toy puppy head dangled over his face, and when he crawled on all fours it looked pretty good, almost like he was a real puppy.

At my signal, Boss Baby crawled out from under the game booth and started moving toward the doggy door. A little girl thought he was a real dog and picked him up, but he bit her arm and she let him go.

"I've never been so humiliated in my life," Boss Baby grumbled.

Then he turned around to see a bunch of real puppies sniffing his butt.

Boss Baby was almost to the doggy door.

"Arf," he said, when he passed the guard.

The guard thought he was a real puppy. I held my breath as Boss Baby approached the doggy door . . .

Just then a new batch of puppies burst through

it from the other side! They tackled Boss Baby, licking him and playing with him.

I grabbed the ball from the game booth and tossed it to the puppies. They ran away from Boss Baby and chased the ball.

Boss Baby was on his feet now, and he ran for the door. That made the guard suspicious, and he picked up Boss Baby.

Boss Baby grimaced, but he started to lick the guard's face. The guard dropped him and went to the water fountain to wash off. Boss Baby dove through the doggy door, and since the guard was distracted, I made a dash for the door too. I slipped through just in time.

We made it! We were inside Puppy Co!

# Chapter 11
## Francis Francis

"Timothy Templeton, office ninja!" I cried as Boss Baby and I made our way down an empty hallway. My heart was pounding. Our mission was off to an exciting start.

"Shhh!" Boss Baby warned me.

He stopped in front of a door that read: KEEP OUT! NO KIDS ALLOWED.

"It's almost like it's begging us to go in," Boss Baby said suspiciously.

We pushed open the door.

The room inside was dark. We shone our flashlights around and saw some tables and chairs. The door behind us creaked shut.

"This is getting creepy," I said.

Then a spotlight shone on a box stacked on top of a short pedestal.

"That's it! The file!" Boss Baby cried.

We ran up to it. There was a file folder on top of the box, labeled: NEW PUPPY—TOP SECRET.

Boss Baby reached for it, but I slapped his hand away.

"No, I've seen this before somewhere," I said. I think it was a movie. The adventure guy knew that if he picked up the statue he was stealing, an alarm would go off. So he had to replace the statue with something the exact same weight. "We've got to find something to replace it with."

Boss Baby nodded. "You're right, like another file?"

I nodded, and he picked up a file laying on top of another box. "Smead manila. Pressboard edges. About fifty ounces. Wait, no . . ." He took one page out of the file. "49 ounces. Try this one."

I took it from him and got ready to make the switch.

"Wait!" Boss Baby said. He took a paper clip from his jacket pocket and placed it carefully on the replacement folder. "Now it's perfect."

I held the fake file in my left hand, and placed

my right hand over the real file. I had to make the switch at the exact same time. Boss Baby stood next to me, watching. He was so excited that he was starting to drool.

I took a deep breath . . . and switched them. No alarm went off! I had done it!

Boss Baby grabbed the file from me and stared at it. But a drop of drool fell from his mouth onto the fake file. The pedestal under the box began to sink into the floor.

"Uh-oh," I said.

"Oops," said Boss Baby.

We had triggered some kind of trap! The lights came on and we saw that we were in the middle of some crazy kind of machine. A paddle knocked into a boot, and the boot kicked a bucket that dumped a ball down a slide. Then the ball hit a lever, and a bathtub came up from the floor.

"I feel like we should run," I said.

"I know, but it's just so mesmerizing," said Boss Baby.

I nodded. "I kinda want to see how it ends."

"Yeah, me too," he agreed.

The ball kept rolling. It rolled down a hole and landed on a seesaw. Sitting on the other end of the seesaw was the guy in the puppy costume—Puppy Co. Pete! He launched through the air and landed in the tub. Water splashed, and a cage fell from the ceiling and crashed down around Boss Baby and me.

"Well, that didn't end well," Boss Baby said. He opened up the secret file. There was a piece of paper inside with one word:

GOTCHA!

Then Puppy Co. Pete started to laugh. A trapdoor opened underneath us, and Boss Baby and I dropped down through the floor. We each landed in a soft chair shaped like a puppy. Each puppy's arms closed around us, locking us into place. Puppy Co. Pete dropped down from the ceiling too, but he didn't get locked into a chair like we did.

Then a black leather office chair swirled around, revealing a guy in a business suit.

"You're right on time," he said.

"Francis Francis?" I couldn't believe it.

"I see you've met my big brother, Eugene," he said, pointing to Puppy Co. Pete. Eugene took off his puppy head to reveal his human face.

"What is all this?" Boss Baby asked.

Francis Francis laughed. "Perhaps you recognize me from my youth!"

He pulled a rope, separating two curtains behind him to reveal a painting of a really, really fat baby in a business suit.

Boss Baby's eyes got big. Really big. "Super Colossal Big Fat Boss Baby?"

"Whoa, he is . . . him?" I asked. "And him is you?"

Francis Francis nodded.

"How did you end up here?" Boss Baby asked in disbelief.

"You know what I do to little kids who ask lots of questions about me?" he asked. "Eugene!"

Eugene ripped off his puppy costume and took a book out of the pocket of his business suit.

"I read them my story," Francis said. "Eugene, my chair!"

Eugene lowered his big body to form a chair, and Francis Francis hopped into his lap. Then he opened his storybook and began to read: "A long, long time ago, I was a hot-shot executive, headed straight to the top! They gave me a promotion . . . the corner office . . . my very own—"

Boss Baby cut him off. "Personal potty?"

The picture of the shiny potty in the storybook said it all.

"Everyone loved me!" continued Francis Francis. "I had it all. The whole pie. And then, one day, I got called in to see the board of directors."

"Who are the boring directors?" I asked.

"The biggest baby bosses of them all," Francis Francis replied. "I thought they loved me, but I was wrong. They replaced me with someone new."

"That's horrible!" I cried.

"Yes, Tim, it was," Francis Francis said. "All of a sudden, she got all the love. All the attention. You know how that feels, don't you, Tim? It hurts, doesn't it?"

I looked at Boss Baby and then I turned back to

Francis Francis. "Yeah . . . it does. And then what happened?"

"I learned that babies are selfish, greedy little creatures," he went on. "They fired me and took away my special formula. Then they sent me down to live with a f-family!"

But Francis Francis had a plan.

"Baby Corp. stole all the love from me, and now I'm going to take it back with . . . the Forever Puppy."

He flipped to the next page of his book and showed us a picture of the cutest puppy ever! But he didn't stop there. He showed us a picture of the puppy with a baby. In the next picture, the baby was a toddler, but the puppy was still a puppy. The next picture showed that the baby had grown into a kid my age—and the puppy was still a puppy. He kept flipping, and the kid became a grown-up, but the puppy stayed the same!

"Imagine a puppy that never gets old," Francis Francis said. "Never grows up. A puppy that stays a puppy forever. It'll be so adorable! Once I launch my Forever Puppies, no one will ever love a baby ever again! The end of babies . . . the end of Baby Corp.!"

"Ha!" Boss Baby said. "A puppy that never grows up is impossible."

Eugene grabbed my backpack.

Francis Francis grinned. "You're right," he said. "Why, you'd need some sort of . . . youth formula."

Eugene took Boss Baby's bottle out of my backpack.

"My super secret baby formula!" Boss Baby cried.

Francis Francis was delighted. "You walked right into my trap. You brought me the very thing I needed to make the Forever Puppy a reality! I mean, who would actually take children to a place of business?"

"I knew it!" cried Boss Baby. "You were my hero. How could you do this? How could you betray your company?"

"Baby Corp. betrayed me!" Francis Francis said.

"You'll never get away with this," Boss Baby said.

"Oh, but I will," Francis Francis said confidently. He pushed a button on his desk. A screen on the wall lit up, showing my parents in the lobby. They were looking for me and Boss Baby!

"I'm taking them both with me to Las Vegas," Francis Francis said. "So stay out of my way. I'd hate for them to get fired."

That didn't sound good. But I knew something that Francis Francis didn't.

"They'd never leave us alone," I said.

"Oh, really?" Francis Francis asked. "Wait until they meet Puppy Co.'s certified in-house childcare expert."

He nodded toward Eugene. In the blink of an eye, the big guy was suddenly wearing a dress! And there was a gray wig on his head! He looked like some kind of weird grandma.

"Oh no!" I groaned.

## Chapter 12
## Bad Nanny

Everything happened so fast after that. It seemed like right after we got home it was time for my parents to leave on their business trip. The three of us—me, Boss Baby, and Eugene in his nanny disguise—stood in the front yard to see them off. Francis Francis was there too.

"Don't be nervous, buddy," Dad told me. "We'll be back before you know it."

"It's only overnight," Mom added. "Besides, you boys are in great hands."

"That's right!" Francis Francis said. "Eugenia is practically perfect in every way. Believe me, she won't take her eyes off your children," he said. "Not for one second."

There was nothing I could do to warn my parents. Luggage was thrown into the trunk, doors were slammed, and they were off.

"To the airport!" I could hear Francis Francis instruct the driver.

Eugene brought me and Boss Baby into the house and we immediately escaped to his room.

Boss Baby started pacing back and forth, like he does when he's thinking.

"It's over! I'm through!" he said anxiously. Then his watch beeped. It was time for more super secret baby formula, but Francis Francis had stolen it.

"Without that formula, I start turning into a normal baby!" Boss Baby explained. "You know, goo-goo, ga-ga, the whole bit! What do we do, Templeton? What do we do?"

"We have to get to the airport and stop Francis Francis before the plane takes off!" I said.

"Yes, but how do we get past that evil nanny down there?" Boss Baby asked. Then his eyes filled with tears, and he started to cry—like a real baby!

"Okay, let me think," I said, and then Boss Baby suddenly started to laugh.

Boss Baby rolled over and put his foot in his mouth.

"What's going on?" I asked.

Boss Baby jumped up, snapping back to reality, and started to scream. "Ahh! Don't look at me! I'm going full baby!"

"Oh no!" I cried.

"Ugh! I'm a ticking baby time bomb!" Boss Baby started to panic. Drool was dangling out of his mouth. "I'm going to turn into a puking, pooping, helpless baby."

Then it hit me. "Wait, that's great!"

"How is that great?" he asked.

"I know exactly what to do," I replied.

I quickly put my plan into action. Eugene was in the living room, watching a cooking show. I snuck down into the kitchen and got some jars of baby food and the vacuum cleaner. Then I went back upstairs and took some of Mom's makeup. I put green eye makeup all over Boss Baby's face, and stuck some macaroni to it.

Then I carried Boss Baby downstairs.

"The baby! I think he's sick!" I cried. "You gotta do something!"

Eugene looked over at Boss Baby's green, gross face and screamed.

Then I reversed the switch on the vacuum cleaner so it threw things out instead of sucking them in and spewed a bunch of baby food at Eugene. I hid the machine behind me, so it looked like Boss Baby was throwing up! The baby food got all over Eugene's face.

"Gross, it got in your mouth!" I yelled. Then I turned Boss Baby toward me and turned the vacuum cleaner on again. I sprayed the fake puke all over my face.

"Ew! It got in my mouth too! I think I'm gonna be sick!"

Eugene gagged and ran out of the living room, toward the bathroom. He leaned over the toilet, and Boss Baby sent the vacuum crashing into him! Eugene's head fell into the toilet, and the lid banged on top of his head! Then Boss Baby closed the door behind him.

We high-fived in triumph, but we didn't have any time to spare. Boss Baby and I ran to the garage and jumped onto my bike. We put on helmets. I hit the button and the garage door opened—and we took off.

I pedaled as hard as I could, but I used training wheels, and I couldn't go very fast. I looked behind me and saw Eugene running after us! The toilet lid was stuck to his head.

"Toodooloo, toilet head!" Boss Baby called out.

Eugene got angry and smashed the toilet. Then he charged after us. I didn't think we could outrun him!

Boss Baby held up a dinosaur walkie-talkie. I heard it crackling.

"Staci, I'm being chased by an evil babysitter!" Boss Baby said. "Code red! Gather the team!"

I glanced behind us. Staci and Jimbo appeared, riding Staci's flower bike. The triplets drove their mini fire truck. They rolled right in front of Eugene.

"Huh?" Eugene was confused.

Jimbo jumped up onto Eugene's back and started rolling his popper toy all over Eugene's face! Eugene growled and broke the toy.

"Poppy!" Jimbo yelled, and started punching Eugene. Eugene tossed him away.

Staci rolled up next. She squirted water at Eugene from a plastic flower on her bike. Then the triplets leaped off their fire truck and pounded Eugene with karate kicks. Jimbo ran up and started tickling Eugene's armpits.

We were getting away! But I knew it wouldn't be long before Eugene broke away from those babies.

"Tim, you've got to go faster!" Boss Baby said.

"I can't! I'm just a beginner!" I told him.

"You can do it!" Boss Baby cheered me on. "Now pedal like you mean it!"

I pedaled with all my might, and we were finally breaking away from Eugene. Then something else broke—my training wheels! What had been going so well was now a wobbly mess.

"I can't ride without training wheels!" I wailed. As I swerved down the sidewalk, all hope seemed lost.

Boss Baby started shouting business sayings at me to cheer me on. "Whether you think you can, or you think you can't, you're right."

"What are you talking about?" I yelled back at him, but he kept on going and I kept on pedaling.

"The path to success is not a straight line, Templeton, but rather a wild ride, like a ship at sea! And you're a sea captain, taming a turbulent ocean!"

"I'm a sea captain, taming the ocean," I repeated, reassuring myself. I kept pushing on. I pedaled to a steep hill and then the bike sped down really fast! I saw a limousine ahead.

"There they are! Mom and Dad!" I yelled.

"You did it!" Boss Baby cheered.

"No, we did it," I told him.

"And all without your training wheels," Boss Baby said.

It was a nice moment, but we hadn't saved the day yet.

## Chapter 13
## Stop That Plane!

Boss Baby and I rode through the crowded airport on my bike. We had to get to my parents before their plane took off. We looked through the crowd and spotted them on the floor above us!

I ditched the bike and ran toward the escalator with Boss Baby toddling behind me.

I got to the escalator and started running up it. When I looked behind me, I saw Boss Baby sitting on the floor! He was acting like a real baby, clapping his hands and playing with some coins he had found.

I knew it was because his super secret baby formula was still wearing off. I hesitated. I had to get to my parents—but I couldn't leave a helpless baby in the middle of an airport, could I?

I ran down the escalator and scooped up Boss Baby just before some lady in high heels stepped on him. Then I ran as fast as I could back up the escalator, and down the long path where my parents had gone. It wasn't easy, because Boss Baby was pretty heavy.

By the time I got to the boarding gate, Mom and Dad were about to go through the long tube thing that leads to the plane. Francis Francis was right next to them.

"Mom! Dad!" I yelled.

"Tim?" Dad said in disbelief.

"What are you doing here?" Mom asked.

"Don't get on that plane!" I yelled, but it was too late. Francis Francis motioned to two Puppy Co. security guards and they pushed my parents into the tube.

"No! Stop! Wait!" I yelled, but the door closed behind them. I tried to open it, but it was locked.

Boss Baby and I ran to the window. The plane was starting to roll away.

"Stop!" I yelled, but nobody paid attention to me. I was just a little kid. Mom and Dad watched from the window, but they were as helpless as I was.

Soon, the plane took off and lifted high into the sky.

I sank to the floor. "They're gone."

"I failed. We're never going to stop the launch in time," Boss Baby said.

I couldn't believe that was what Boss Baby was worried about. "What? Who cares?" I barked. "My parents are in danger."

"I care. Baby Corp. is going to go out of business!" Boss Baby said.

We started to argue. "They're my *family*!" I said.

"It's my *company*!" Boss Baby replied.

"Ugh! That's all you ever talk about. You don't even know what it's like to be part of a family," I told him.

"And you don't know what it's like to have a job!" he said.

But I wasn't finished. "You don't know anything about hugs, or bedtime stories, or special songs! You don't know anything about love!"

"Oh, please. Stop acting like a baby," he shot back.

"*You're* a baby!" I yelled.

Boss Baby gasped. "You take that back."

But I wouldn't. "No! This is your fault. Everything was perfect until you showed up!"

"Oh, believe me, kid, the feeling is mutual," he said. "I wish I'd never met you!"

"You ruined my life," I told him. "I wish you'd never been born!"

Boss Baby looked sad when I said that. He straightened his tie and started to walk away.

"Where are you going?" I asked.

But Boss Baby just continued walking. I felt so hopeless. I sat there against the wall, staring straight ahead, for a long time. Then I heard an announcement over the airport speaker system.

"Would Timothy Templeton please pick up the white courtesy phone? Timothy Leslie Templeton, please pick up the white courtesy phone."

I thought that was weird, but I saw a white phone nearby and picked it up.

"It's me. Don't hang up, Tim!" It was Boss Baby's voice.

"Tim, I wasn't born. I was hired. Baby Corp.

is the only home I've ever known," Boss Baby explained. "The whole family thing is kind of new to me. So you're right—I don't know what it's like to be part of a family, but I do care."

I was surprised to hear that. "You do?"

"Yeah, I care about my company the same way you care about your family," Boss Baby said. "And the only way to save both is to stop Francis Francis."

"I can't do this without you, Tim," Boss Baby told me. "I need you."

"I guess we do make a pretty good team," I admitted.

"No, literally . . . I can't reach the doorknobs," Boss Baby reminded me, and I laughed.

"But how do we get to Vegas now?" I asked.

"We're going to need a miracle," Boss Baby answered.

And at that moment, we saw a group of guys dressed up like Elvis walking through the terminal. I don't know a lot about Vegas, but I know that's where all the Elvis impersonators live—and that's where they were probably going.

"Follow that Elvis!" Boss Baby commanded, and I hung up the phone. We quickly found each other and followed the Elvis impersonators. A whole bunch of them were about to board a plane to Las Vegas!

I spotted one of them going into a bathroom, and I had an idea. Boss Baby was thinking the same thing. We borrowed his clothes (okay, we took them, but Boss Baby gave him a bunch of money). Boss Baby climbed onto my shoulders so that we were as tall as a grown-up. Then we put on the costume. Boss Baby's head stuck out on top, and my face was inside the costume.

When we got to the ticket taker, who was also an Elvis impersonator, we didn't have a ticket. But Boss Baby had a plan.

"Oh no! It's been nabbed by some bandito," Boss Baby said.

"Impersonating an Elvis impersonator? That ain't right!" the ticket taker said.

"There he goes!" Boss Baby said, pointing.

The ticket taker turned to look, and Boss Baby and I quickly slid out of the costume. We hurried onto the plane on our hands and knees. Then we lied and told the flight attendant that we were the kids of the plane's pilot! She gave us seats in first class, all the snacks we could eat, and we had a sweet flight to Las Vegas.

To pass the time, I imagined that I was a pirate. My sleep mask became an eye patch. A candy dispenser turned into Francis Francis.

"Aye, all right, Francis Francis," I began in my best pirate voice. "This will teach you to kidnap the parents of one-eyed Tim." I knocked the candy dispenser over.

Boss Baby wasn't impressed. "Oh, please. If only it were that easy."

"Well, what's your plan?" I asked him. "You're not going to write a memo, are you?"

"Uh," he said, crumpling up a piece of paper. "No."

"Come on. You said you never really had a childhood, right?" I handed the candy dispenser to him. "Why don't you give it a try?"

So he could have an eye patch too, we covered

his eye with his tie. "Go on, say something mean to him," I encouraged.

"You have the guts to ask me for a bonus now? Ha!" he said.

"Now you're getting into it!" I told him. We both looked down and saw that our clothes had turned into full pirate outfits and there were enemy pirates swarming in.

Together, Boss Baby and I fought them off. He was swashbuckling with the best of them.

"You're fired! And here's your severance package! Ha!" Boss Baby cried as the last pirate went overboard.

It was a great moment, but something wasn't quite right. "You're not supposed to end with 'Ha!'" I explained. "You're supposed to end with 'AAARRRGH!'"

Boss Baby was a fast learner. "AAARRRGH!!" he cried. It was perfect.

Before we knew it, we were on the ground in Las Vegas and exiting the plane with a bunch of Elvis

impersonators. And that's when we saw him . . .
Eugene, also dressed up like Elvis! We quickly
hightailed it away from him and out of the busy airport terminal.

We got a ride to the convention center where the
Pet Conference was being held. The car dropped
us off and we ran inside. The first thing I noticed
was how enormous this place was. It was even
more crowded than the airport. It was filled with
booths from all kinds of pet companies, featuring
pet toys, pet beds, pet food, pet clothes, and actual
pets. An enormous setup of colorful giant hamster
tubes snaked around the whole place. The sound of
barking, chirping, and meowing rose above all the
talking people. How would we ever find my parents?

## Chapter 14
# The Big Launch

Luckily, I spotted a big board with the names of all the companies on it. I ran over and read through the list. I quickly spotted Puppy Co., and saw where the Puppy Co. stage was on the map.

I turned around to tell Boss Baby. He had waddled over to a glittery cat toy display and was back in real baby mode, cooing and drooling.

"Not again!" I said, picking him up. Then I moved my backpack from my back to my front and stuffed him inside so he wouldn't wander off again.

I spun around to head to the Puppy Co. stage—and I saw that man of disguise, Eugene, across the room! He was still dressed like Elvis.

Eugene started running toward me, so I ran into the cheering crowd. Francis Francis was up on stage. He began to speak as my parents brought out a giant heart-shaped box.

"Ladies and gentlemen, imagine a puppy that never grows up. Never gets old. A puppy that stays a puppy forever. I give you the only thing you'll ever love—the Forever Puppy!"

Francis Francis opened a big heart-shaped present and a Forever Puppy looked out. The crowd went wild. Even I started to feel mesmerized by its cuteness.

"Avert your eyes, Templeton," Boss Baby commanded. And that's when Francis Francis noticed his brother in the back of the crowd.

"What are you doing here?" Francis Francis barked at Eugene.

Eugene simply pointed to us. I was calling to Mom and Dad.

"What are *they* doing here?" Francis Francis barked even louder.

"What are Tim and the baby doing here?" Dad asked, finally noticing us.

Francis Francis tried to play it cool for the crowd watching him. "What are any of us doing here, really?"

But Dad wasn't buying it. "What's going on here?" he demanded.

Francis Francis knew he had to do something, so he pushed my parents into the heart-shaped box!

"Get them!" Francis Francis ordered Eugene, and he started coming toward us.

Meanwhile, Francis Francis started pushing the box with my parents inside backstage.

"Tim, we've got to get backstage!" cried Boss Baby.

"In there!" I said, pointing to a giant hamster trail that led off the stage.

We crawled inside the tube. Eugene followed us, but he was too big. Soon, he was stuck in the tube.

Boss Baby and I crawled as quickly as we could.

Below us, through the clear tube, we could see a big platform. Regular puppies were being carried down a line that ran from the ceiling over a vat marked SUPER SECRET BABY FORMULA. Each puppy had a little parachute on. When they were above the vat, the puppies were sprayed with the formula, becoming Forever Puppies. Then a conveyor belt carried them into a huge rocket. Through the rocket windows, we could see thousands of Forever Puppies inside! Once the countdown was over, the rocket would launch into the sky. The plan was that Forever Puppies would parachute safely down all over the world.

"Now that's how you launch a product," Boss Baby quipped.

Then I spotted something else. Francis Francis had put the heart-shaped box under the rocket. My parents were still inside!

Suddenly the tube began to shake. I turned around and saw that Eugene was trying to break out of the tube.

*Snap!* He broke it, and we all started to fall.

"Aaaaaaahhhhhh!" Boss Baby and I both screamed.

Eugene landed in a giant kitty litter display filled with cats. The cats pounced on him immediately. That would occupy him for the time being. I grabbed on to another tube and stopped our fall. Then Boss Baby and I dropped onto a platform hanging down from the ceiling. The rocket was still far below us.

"Mom! Dad! I'm coming!" I yelled.

I ran across the platform to some metal stairs that went down to the rocket launching pad. But then Francis Francis was there and blocked the stairway!

"I'm launching that rocket and there's nothing you can do about it," Francis Francis threatened.

"No!" I yelled.

He kept coming toward me, and I backed up slowly. "Baby Corp. stole all the love from me, and now I'm going to take it back from them. You should understand what I'm talking about! You got replaced just like me!"

I stopped and looked right at him. "No, I'm nothing like you!"

"Let our parents go!" Boss Baby added. "His parents. The parents."

"Yeah!" I shouted.

Francis Francis looked at me. "You could have had your parents' love all to yourself again, but no, you blew it. You let that baby boss you around."

Boss Baby wasn't having any of this. "He doesn't work for me. We're partners!"

He noticed a pacifier cord dangling from Francis Francis's pocket. He grabbed it and handed it to me. I knew just what to do with it. I shoved it into Francis Francis's mouth. For the first time in many years, that big baby was back at Baby Corp. It was just what we needed to escape. I started running away, but Francis Francis wasn't out for long.

The pacifier fell out of his mouth, and he threw it at my legs like a lasso. It hit me, and I slipped! I nearly fell off the platform, but I grabbed on to the railing just in time. With my other hand, I caught Boss Baby. My legs were dangling over the edge.

"Baby Corp. is through!" Francis Francis cheered. "I win! Ha!"

"Wrong!"

Boss Baby glared at Francis Francis. "You're not supposed to say, 'Ha!,'" he said. Boss Baby reached out with his pointer. It had turned into a pirate sword.

"That's right!" I said.

"You're supposed to end with . . . ," Boss Baby began.

"AAARRGGH!" we said together and jumped back up on the platform.

All three of us were suddenly wearing pirate outfits. I threw Boss Baby up on my shoulders and we started walking toward Francis Francis. This time he was the one backing up, afraid.

"You're fired!" I shouted.

"And here's your severance package!" added Boss Baby, and he grabbed Francis Francis by his tie. Then he tossed him off the platform.

*Plop!* He landed in the big vat of super secret baby formula.

"Take that, you scurvy scallywag!" I yelled down below.

And that's when I heard Mom and Dad yell. They were still in the heart-shaped box underneath the rocket.

"Help!"

"Anybody!"

The launch countdown boomed over the speakers. *"One minute and counting . . ."*

I looked at the long, long flight of stairs leading to the rocket. We'd never make it to my parents in time. Or would we?

## Chapter 15
# We're in This Together

We couldn't give up now. I had to think of something!

We were right next to the line that carried the puppies down into the vat of super secret baby formula. I knew what I had to do. Boss Baby went into my backpack again, and I grabbed one of the puppies off the line.

Then I jumped off the platform.

"What are you doing?" Boss Baby screamed.

The puppy's parachute opened right above the rocket. We glided down to the floor safely.

"Mom and Dad! I'm coming!" I yelled.

"Tim, are you okay?" Dad asked.

"Is the baby all right?" Mom added.

"Yes, the baby's fine," Boss Baby answered in his deep voice.

Luckily, my parents couldn't see him. "Who was that?" Mom asked.

"Um, that was me," I said.

I tried to unlock the box, but the lock wouldn't budge. The Forever Puppies inside the rocket were barking like crazy.

I looked around, trying to think of a solution. Then I spotted the way out of this mess.

"Hey, I know a way to move my parents," I said. I pointed up to the emergency hatch on top of the rocket. "We can use the puppies."

Boss Baby nodded. "Upsies! I need upsies!"

The launch countdown went off again.

*"T-minus forty-five seconds."*

I grabbed Boss Baby and tossed him as hard as I could. He landed on the window of the emergency hatch. Like a superhero, he climbed up to the handle and released the hatch.

The door lowered, and a wave of Forever Puppies poured out! They pushed me and the box out from underneath the rocket. Then the puppies ran away from the rocket, and we bounced along on top of their backs.

"We're moving!" Mom yelled.

"Why are we moving?" Dad asked.

"All right, Mom and Dad!" I cheered. "Hang on!"

We were safe! I was so happy!

Then I remembered—where was Boss Baby?

I looked up. Boss Baby was still high up on the rocket! He was dangling from the door.

*"T-minus thirty seconds."*

I had to save Boss Baby. I dove under the puppies and crawled to the rocket.

"Go, Tim!" Boss Baby yelled. "Get your parents out of here!"

Then his eyes got big, and he started to coo and drool. He was back to acting like a baby again!

"You've got to jump!" I yelled, but Boss Baby just smiled.

"Come on, it's a piece of cake!" I shouted, but Boss Baby just started moving his hands like he was playing patty cake.

"No! We don't have any time for patty cake. Get down!" I yelled again.

*"Twenty seconds."*

The rocket started to shake as it got ready to take off. Poor Boss Baby was going to get launched into space, and I couldn't help him. I started to cry. Boss Baby saw me and started to cry too.

*"Fifteen seconds!"*

Boss Baby was wailing now. I had to figure out a way to get him to jump down. But how could I get him to calm down first?

I thought about how Mom and Dad used to get me to calm down. Suddenly, I knew what to do. I started to sing the bedtime song.

*"Little bird, don't you cry, one day you will learn to fly. . . ."*

Boss Baby stopped crying. I kept singing. The clock kept counting.

*"Five . . . four . . ."*

*"Fly, little bird, fly,"* I sang. I held out my arms. Boss Baby looked down at me.

*"Three . . . two . . . one . . ."*

And then, he took a step, right off the rocket.

*"Zero. Blastoff."*

I caught Boss Baby and ran toward a big concrete

pillar and hid behind it. The rocket blasted off!

"I looked down at Boss Baby. "Are you still in there?"

He put his hand to his mouth. He was still in baby mode. That's when I remembered the vat of super secret baby formula. We ran over to it. Boss Baby opened his mouth and a drop fell in. Like magic, he was back.

"What happened? Did we win?" he asked.

"We won," I told him, and we both started to cheer.

Then a loud cry rang out. Smoke poured from the vat of super secret baby formula, and then cleared.

It was Francis Francis! He crawled out of the vat—but he wasn't a businessman anymore. The formula had turned him back into a fat little baby again.

"You ruined everything! It's not fair! It's not fair!" he yelled. "Now you're really going to pay!"

He ran toward me and Boss Baby, but before he could reach us, Eugene appeared and picked him up.

"Eugene! You put me down! You hear me? I'm

the boss of you!" Francis Francis yelled.

Eugene stuck a pacifier in Francis Francis's mouth. "This time, we'll raise him right," he said, and then he walked off, carrying his little brother with him.

But Boss Baby and I couldn't dwell on the happy moment for too long. My parents were still stuck in the box! Luckily, Boss Baby's arm was small enough to fit inside the lock. He popped it open! Mom and Dad were free!

"Are you okay?" Mom asked.

"We're fine," I assured her.

"You saved us!" said Dad.

"You're our hero," Mom said to me.

"And a great big brother," added Dad.

"We love you both so much," Mom said.

"Both of us?" I asked.

Mom nodded. "With all our heart."

That's when it hit me. Mom and Dad had enough love for both me *and* Boss Baby! I had never needed to worry about that.

"Let's go home," Dad said.

# Chapter 16
# Good-Bye

Boss Baby and I had done it. We had saved my parents and saved Baby Corp. So we both should have been pretty happy, right?

But I really wasn't. Because it was time for Boss Baby to go back to Baby Corp.

He packed all his stuff into his suitcase and called a taxi. I brought him outside.

His team of babies was out there waiting for him.

"Well, team, good job," he addressed them. Then he turned to Staci and handed her a letter of recommendation. "Staci, this should get you into the school of your choice."

Next, he gave the triplets some advice. "It's okay to think for yourself," he told them.

"No sir/No way/That's a terrible idea," they said.

"That's the attitude!" Boss Baby encouraged.

"You're so right/You got it, sir/Absolutely, B.B.," they replied.

Boss Baby just looked up at me and rolled his eyes. I laughed.

Then it was time to say good-bye to Jimbo. Boss Baby had something special for him: a cookie. "Here you go, big guy. You've earned it."

Jimbo was so touched he started to cry. He grabbed Boss Baby for a big hug.

"I'll miss you too, buddy!" said Boss Baby. Jimbo finally put him down and the babies started to walk off.

Then it was just me and him.

"Congratulations on your promotion," I said. "The corner office, the private potty, all that stuff."

"But hey, how about you?" Boss Baby asked. "You have your parents all to yourself."

I nodded. It was what I had wanted all along. But now I wasn't so sure.

"So, what am I gonna tell Mom and Dad after you leave?" I asked.

"Don't worry," Boss Baby said. "Baby Corp. has

a procedure for situations like this. It'll be like, uh . . . I was never born."

Like he was never born . . .

"Oh, I almost forgot," Boss Baby said. He reached into his briefcase and pulled out Lam-Lam, all stitched up and good as new.

"No way! You fixed her!" I said.

"Yep. She's a tough one," Boss Baby answered.

I started to walk away. Then I looked back at Boss Baby. "Well, I guess we both got what we wanted."

Boss Baby nodded. "It's a win-win."

He walked up to the door of the taxi. Then he stopped. I thought for a minute that he wouldn't leave. But he pointed up to the door handle.

"Oh yeah. Right," I said, and I opened the door for him and helped him hop in.

"Tim, thanks for everything," Boss Baby said.

"You're welcome," I said.

Then I waved to Boss Baby as the taxi cab drove away.

# Chapter 17
# A Job Offer

I walked into my house to find that a bunch of Baby Corp. workers came and got rid of everything that was Boss Baby's. Every toy, every pacifier. They used a wand to erase my parents' memories. They offered it to me, but I refused. I wanted to remember Boss Baby.

Over the next few days, I thought that might have been a big mistake. I missed Boss Baby like crazy. I missed the cute way he drooled. I missed our adventures together.

Sure, Boss Baby had a big promotion. But maybe I could offer him a better job. I wrote him a letter.

Dear Boss Baby,

I don't usually write very much, but now I know that

memos are very important things. You see, I was wrong. We both were. It turns out there's plenty of love to go around. And to prove it to you, I want to give you all mine.

Maybe it doesn't matter how much love you get. What matters is how much love you give. And you can't measure that on a pie chart.

I would like to offer you a job. It will be hard work and there will be no pay. But the good news is that you can never be fired.

And I promise you this: Every morning when you wake up, I will be there. Every night at dinner, I will be there. Every birthday party, every Christmas morning, I will be there. Year after year after year.

We will grow old together. And you and I will always be brothers.

Always.

I sent the letter to Baby Corp. For a few days, I didn't hear anything. I started to feel sad again. Boss Baby didn't want the job.

Then, one morning, Wizzie woke me up.

"Wake up, little halflings! It's seven a.m.!"

"What's the point, Wizzie?" I asked. But I dragged myself out of bed and looked out the window.

There was no sign of Boss Baby. I turned to go back to bed . . . and then caught a flash of yellow in the corner of my eye.

A taxi cab was turning down my street. It parked in front of my house.

I ran downstairs as fast as I could and opened the front door. Mom and Dad came out of the taxi, and Mom was holding Boss Baby. But he wasn't dressed in a business suit. He was wearing a onesie, and he was cooing and drooling like a normal baby.

"Tim, look who's here," Mom said.

Dad smiled. "It's your new baby—"

"Brother!" I cried, and I picked him up.

Boss Baby smiled up at me.

"You came back! You came back!" I cried happily.

"Say hello to Theodore Lindsey Templeton," Dad said.

"Lindsey?" I repeated, laughing. That was just as bad as Leslie! Boss Baby started to cry.

"Aw, who's ticklish?" I asked, and I tickled his little foot, and he laughed. Mom and Dad wrapped their arms around us for a group hug.

I stared into the eyes of my baby brother. I knew he was going to take over the whole house and boss everyone around, day and night.

And I wouldn't have wanted it any other way.

# Epilogue
# A Happy Ending

*Many years later, when I am grown up . . .*

"So that's my story," I said, closing the family album. I was sitting in the hospital with my daughter, waiting for her baby sister to arrive. "Our story. Luckily for me and my little brother, it had a happy ending."

"Is it a true story, Daddy?" my daughter asked.

"Well, sweetie, that's how I remember it," I told her honestly. "But you know what I found out? There's plenty of love for everyone."